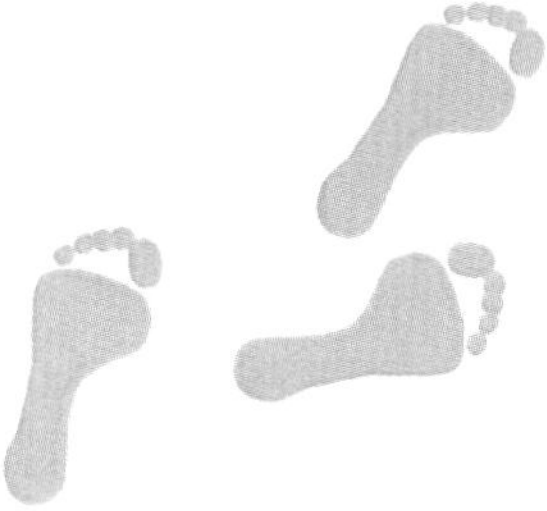

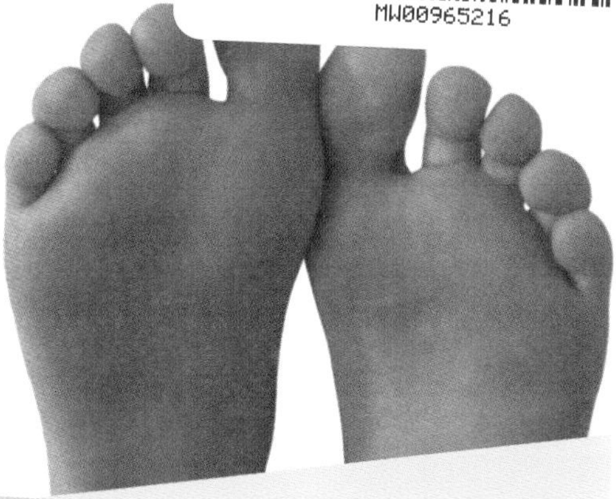

Who Has Toes?

Written by Lynn Bryan

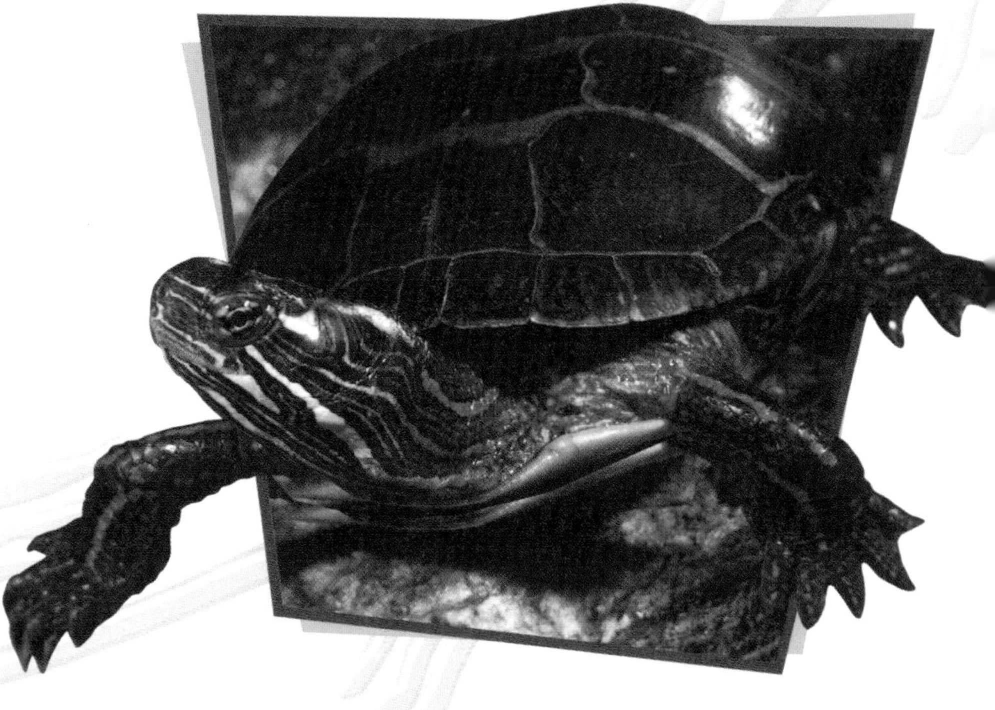

A turtle has toes.

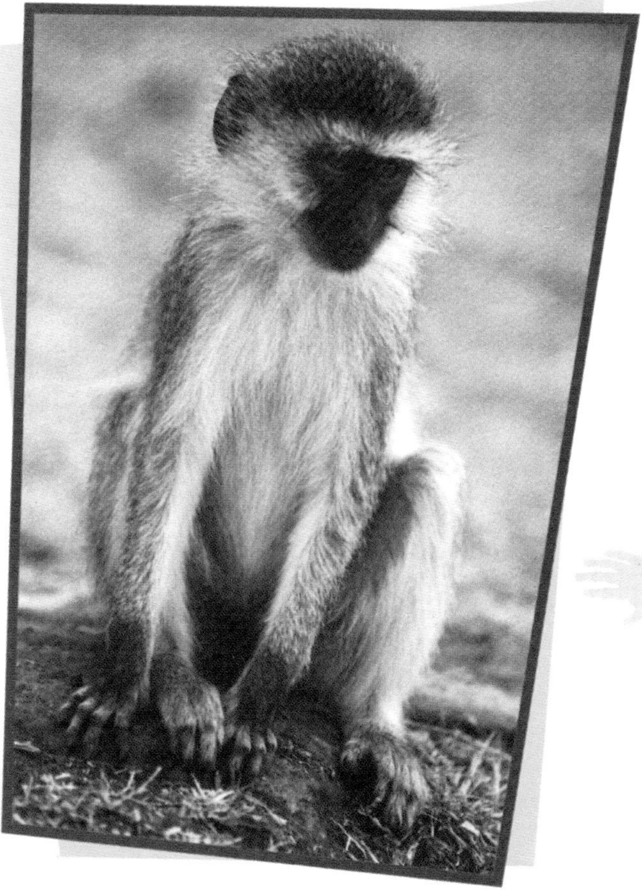

A monkey has toes.

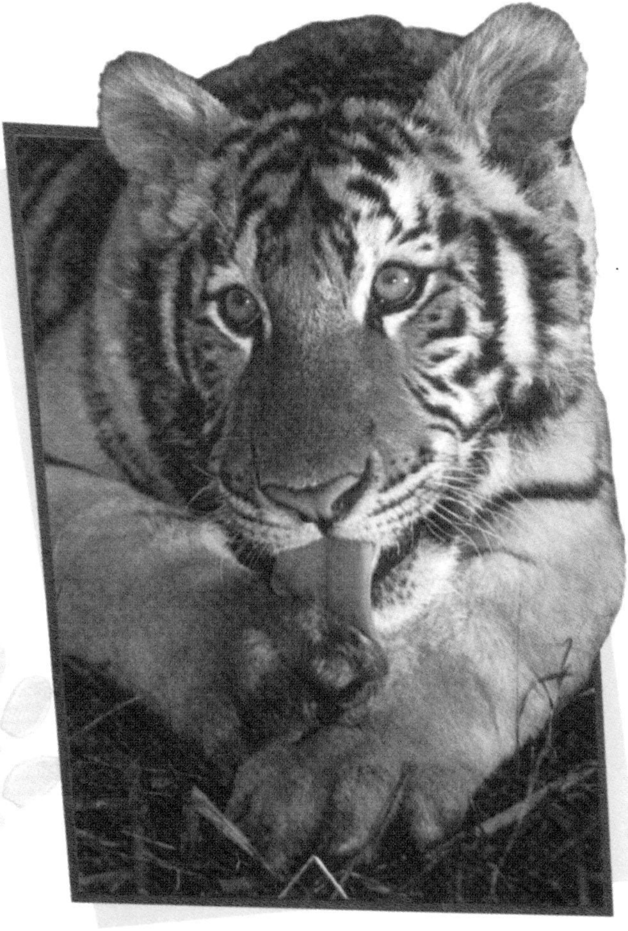

A tiger has toes.

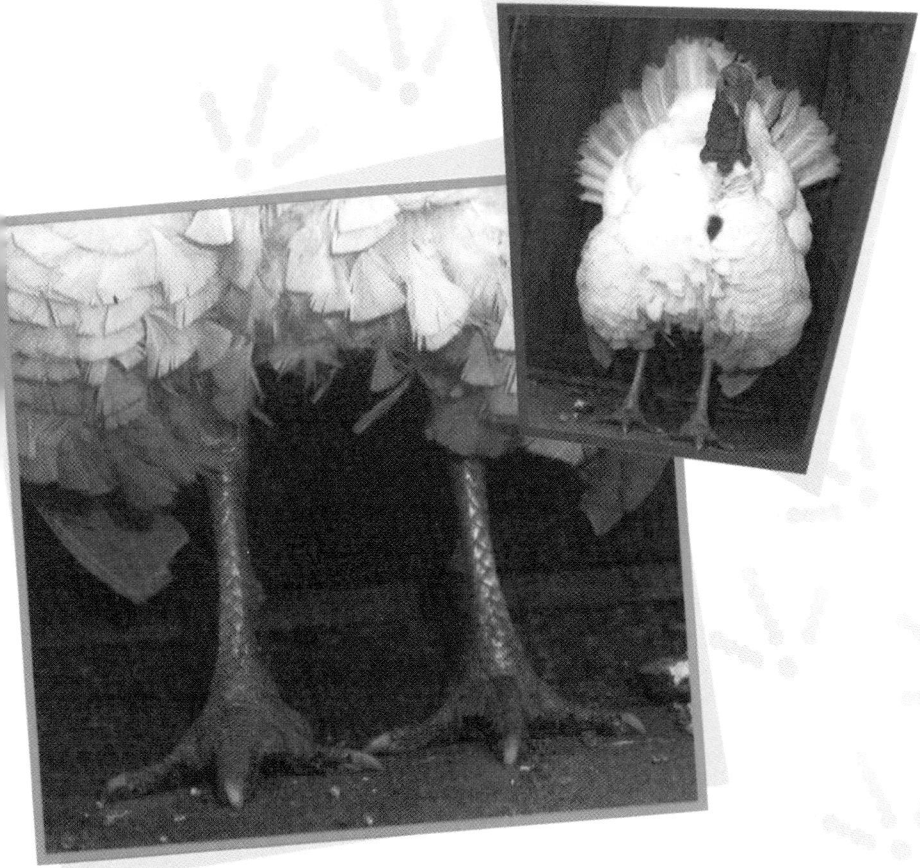

A turkey has toes.

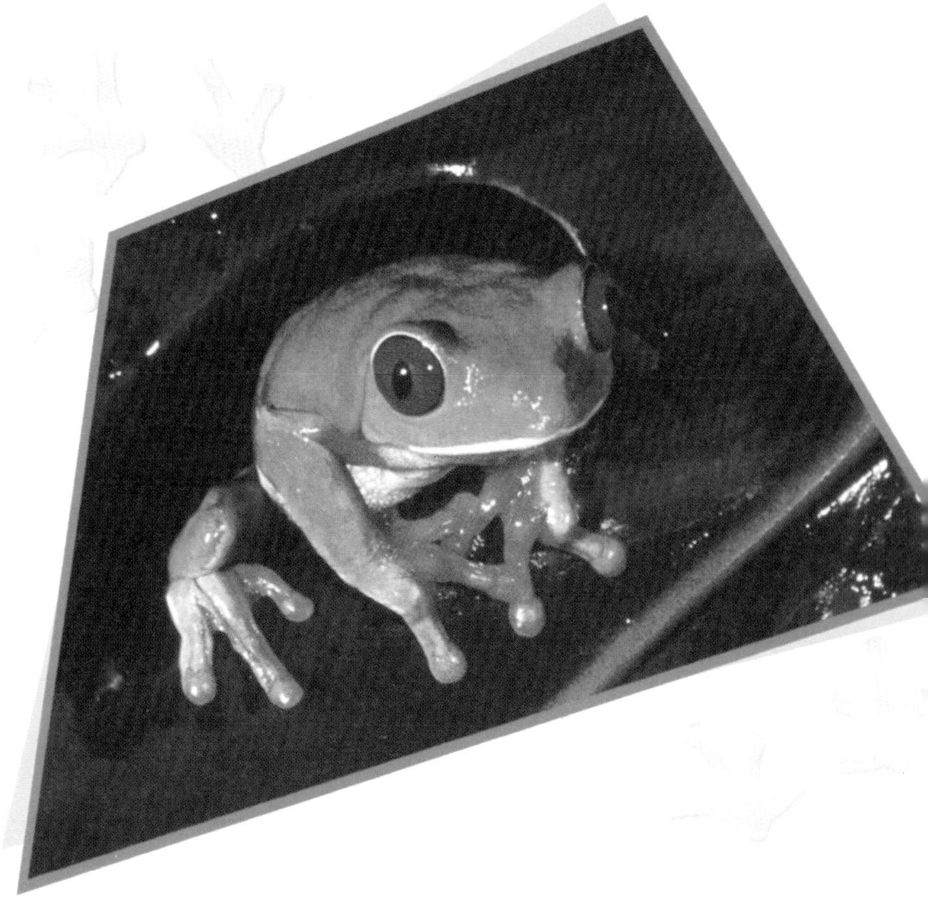

A frog has toes.

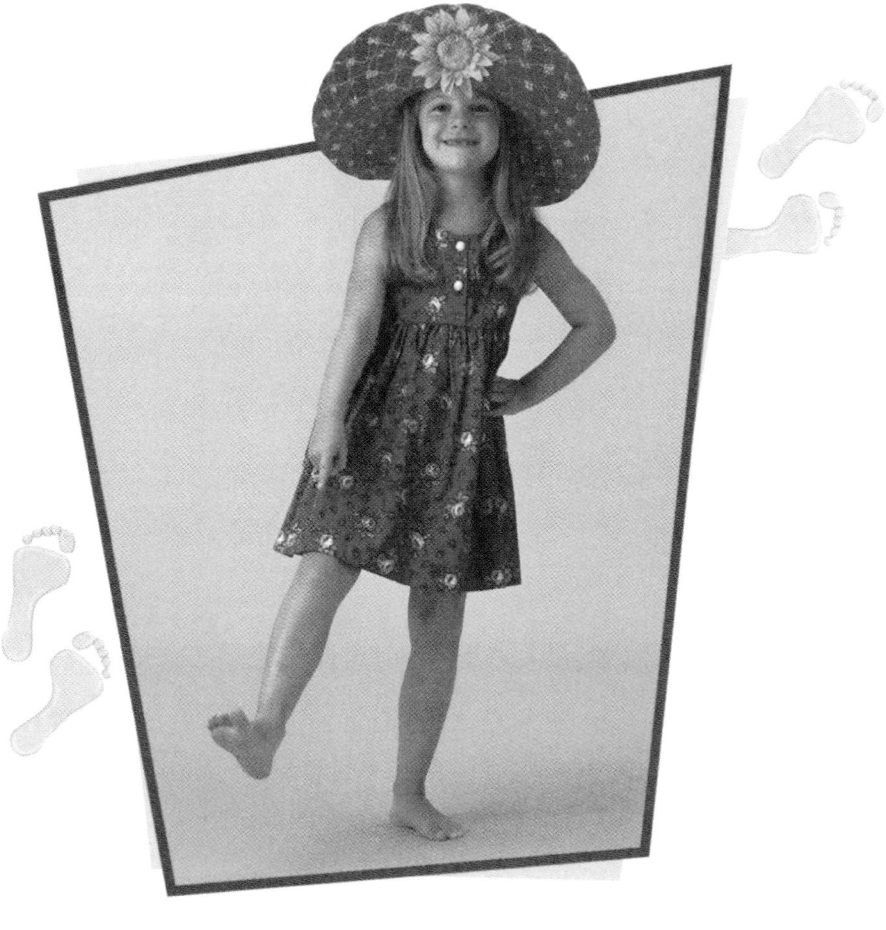

And I have toes too.

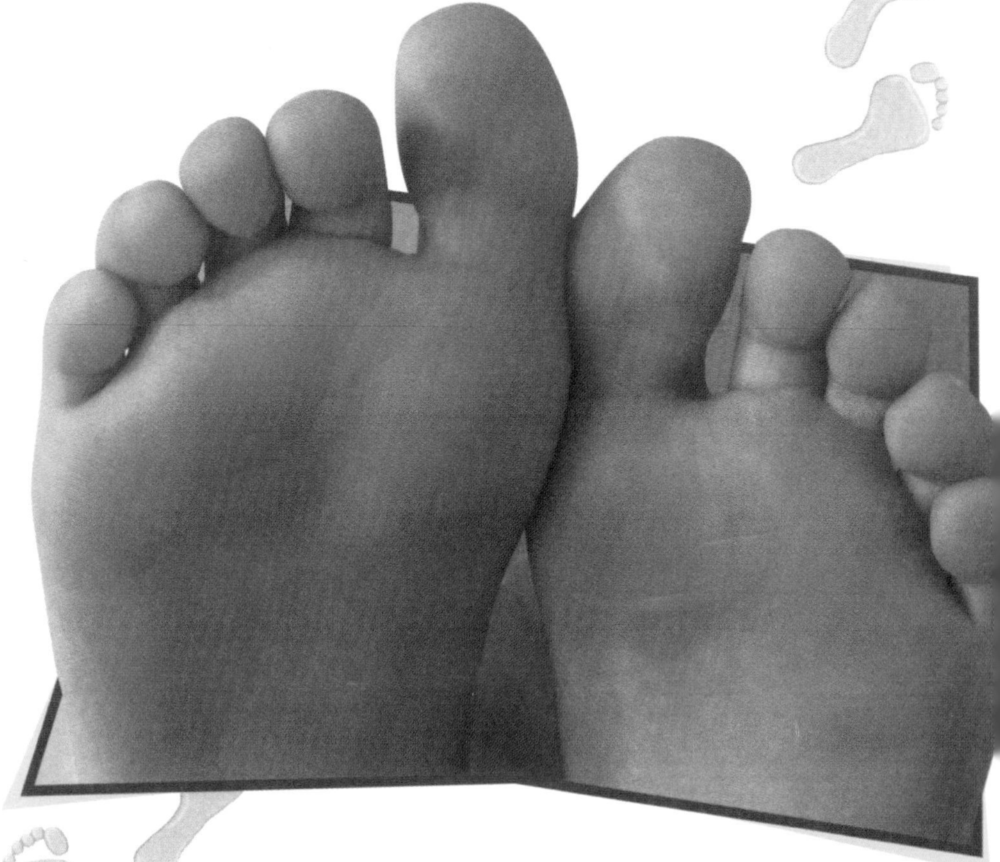

Ten of them!